FAMILY REUNION

FAMILY REUNION

by **Marilyn Singer** • *illustrated by* **R. W. Alley**

Macmillan Publishing Company   New York   Maxwell Macmillan Canada   Toronto
Maxwell Macmillan International   New York   Oxford   Singapore   Sydney

To the distinguished Feingold family—M. S.

To Max, the newest member of our family—R. W. A.

ACKNOWLEDGMENTS
Thanks to Debbie Aronson, Laura Aronson, and Steve
Aronson, and to my editor, Judith Whipple, and all the
folks at Macmillan.

Text copyright © 1994 by Marilyn Singer
Illustrations copyright © 1994 by R. W. Alley
Macmillan
Publishing Company is part of the Maxwell Communica-
tion Group of Companies. Macmillan Publishing Company, 866 Third Avenue, New York, NY 10022. Maxwell
Macmillan Canada, Inc., 1200 Eglinton Avenue East, Suite
200, Don Mills, Ontario M3C 3N1. First edition. Printed in
the United States of America. The text of this book is set
in 13 pt. Berkeley Medium. The illustrations are rendered
in pen and ink and watercolors.
10 9 8 7 6 5 4 3 2 1

Library of Congress Cataloging-in-Publication Data
Singer, Marilyn. Family reunion / by Marilyn Singer ;
illustrated by R. W. Alley. — 1st ed.   p.   cm.
Summary: A series of poems describe the people and
events at a family reunion. ISBN 0-02-782883-2
1. Family reunions—Juvenile poetry. 2. Children's
poetry, American. [1. Family reunions—Poetry.
2. American poetry.]   I. Alley, R. W. (Robert W.), ill.
II. Title. PS3569.I546F36 1994   811'.54—dc20
92-40336

THE NIGHT BEFORE

The night before
        the family reunion
we sit around the TV
        as though it were a crystal ball
begging it to tell us
            will there be rain?
            Thunder loud enough
                to rattle the picnic tables?
            Lightning sharp enough
                to barbecue our burgers?
            Hailstones big enough
                to grand slam right out of the park?

Or will we get lucky
        and see the sun
            rising in the sky
                like a big orange Frisbee
                    that not a soul could catch?

SMALL PARK

SMALL PARK
         says the sign
in letters yellow
         on brown
like squiggles of mustard
            on a hot dog
         slices of lemon
            in a glass of iced tea
This year
            it's my turn to make the joke:
"If the park's so small,
            how are we all going to fit?"

And we laugh

    knowing Small Park

        is the biggest park in town

    big enough to hold mothers, fathers

            grandmas, grandpas
            brothers, sisters
            uncles, aunts
            and cousins, first, second
               and twice-removed

    who come by bus, bicycle

            airplane, auto
            train, scooter
            wheelchair, stroller
            and feet, in hightops, sandals
              and fancy cowboy boots

to share among the tall and shady trees

    what the weatherman got right after all:

        one especially sunny day

            in the middle of August

AUNT ALICIA

Carrie says it's because she was named Alicia
　　　　instead of Alice
Dad declares it's because she was the only girl
　　　　in a house full of boys
Uncle Ned is certain it's her astrological sign—
　　　　Gemini
　　　　　　　　or was it Aquarius?
Well, anyway, here she comes
　　　　in her silk dress
　　　　　　　　blue as the morning glories
　　　　　　　　in the picture Mom let me clip
　　　　　　　　from a catalogue
(While everyone else is in jeans
　　　　　　　　　　and shorts
　　　　　　　　　　playsuits
　　　　　　　　　　and pinafores)

With her white straw hat
　　　　and brown basket
　　　　she sits in the shade
　　　　(While everyone else leaps
　　　　　　　　　　and hops
　　　　　　　　　　rolls
　　　　　　　　　　and tumbles)
and sips papaya juice from a shiny silver thermos
I wish someday she'd startle us
　　　　in sneakers
　　　　　　　　or by climbing up a tree
But then she wouldn't be
　　　　Aunt Alicia

EATING CORN

At lunchtime on the sly
    Frankie and I
        watch everyone eat corn
    keeping track of who's first
        to grab an ear
    and who's last
        who's slow
    and who's fast
There's Aunt Alicia carefully cutting off kernels
    with a knife and fork
Uncle Henry chatting and chomping
    spraying pith and corn juice
        on everyone nearby
Grandma Rita selecting a single small ear
Baby Ben leaving five big buttersticky cobs
    on his plate
        each one missing just one bite

Best of all are the twins
        identical to the eye
But Frankie and I
        can tell them apart
Chucka chucka ding
        goes Peter
                running his teeth up and down the cob
                        like an old-fashioned typewriter carriage
                                flying across the page
While Paul nibbles one kernel at a time
        a one-fingered typist
                searching out every key
Tap pause tap pause tap pause tap tap

FIVE GRANDMAS

"Yo, Grandma," calls Bobby,
     hiding under the table
And five heads turn to look
     everywhere but there
        for the fourth time today
"Who said that?" asks Max's Grandma Deborah,
     pointing her hot dog like a microphone
"I can't imagine," says Carrie's Grandma Anne,
     peering around cross-eyed as a Siamese cat
"Must be a parrot," declares George's Grandma Jane,
     tapping her nose
"Or that other bird, what's its name?"
     wonders Frankie's Grandma Lil,
        checking out the treetops
        for the answer perching there
"A mynah," my Grandma Rita reminds,
     patting her sister on the back.
"That's right," the others all agree,
     and toast themselves with lemonade
While under the table
     Bobby laughs into his knees
        and waits to call "Yo, Grandma"
So five heads will turn
     for the fifth time today

BUG POWER

Max has got bug power
      Tasha and me, we swat and swear
        all around the picnic table
But Max, he sits
      calm as a swami
      muttering words like
        Vespula pennsylvanica
        and *Monomorium minimum*
      to the yellow jackets
        in the soda
      the red ants
        on the cake
      and they never come near him
        not once
Aunt Laura says it's just their names
      in Latin
But I say it's magic
      Latin or not
Because Max has got
      bug power

COUSIN GEORGE

There's one in every family, says Mom
      And I know she means Cousin George
Some people like to play kick ball
      Others enjoy writing poems
But Cousin George, he likes to argue
      Anytime
            Anyplace
                  Anywhere

He'll tell you this flower's a daisy
      when you know it's a dandelion
He'll insist that dog is a poodle
      when you're sure it's a Pekingese
Today, swearing that a cicada
      is a centipede
he gets Max so mad
      that Max drops the bug
      right down his back.

"Look," says Mom
      "He's doing the polka."
"No, no," Uncle Ned disagrees
      "I'm certain it's the waltz."
And for once Cousin George
      wiggling and wriggling
           in his itchy-twitchy dance
doesn't argue with either one of them
doesn't argue at all

HIGH FLY

"Are you good at this game?" Carrie accuses
"Sure," I lie
        standing there in right field
        holding up my brand new glove
                smooth as butterscotch
                and stiff as an old dog's leg
        praying nobody hits one out to me
And nobody does
        until
                bottom of the ninth bases loaded two away
                we're ahead by one
                and uh oh (would you believe?)
            here it comes

"Dare you not to drop it," Carrie teases
Sun-blind I reach
            reach
                and thump (would you believe?)
            here it is

        in the tip-top of my glove

                a snow-cone surprise
Then just like in a really good dream
                there's the cheering
                and the hugging
                and the squeals
And best of all there's Carrie
                with her startled eyes
                    and only her mouth catching flies

SLOW-MOTION SPRINT

It's Uncle Steve's idea

      of course

Uncle Steve

      who likes chess
      and chamber music
      and T'ai Chi—
         this old Chinese exercise
           that makes him look like a man
             dancing underwater

It's after the potato race
      the relay
      the sack hop
      the marathon around the lake
      the hundred-yard dash

when, chuffing and red-faced,

    we surround Cousin Jeff

      who's won every single time

    crying "Unfair! Unfair!"

that Uncle Steve unhurriedly declares,

    "Time for the slow-motion sprint."

Confused, we stare

    till he explains:

        "You have to cross the finish line.
        You have to keep a steady pace.
        You cannot stop or leave or pause.
        The slowest runner wins the race."

We laugh at his rules and his rhyme

    but line up just the same

"One. Two. Three. Go," he says

    dragging out the words

        like a broken-down tape recorder

And we're off

        rabbits trying to be tortoises
        squirrels trying to be snails

and it's hard

    so hard

        inching along like worms in a wheat field
        counting breaths and blades of grass

that in the end

    we no longer care who's the winner

        and we don't even care we don't care

FAMILY BAND

That grouchy time of the afternoon
That cranky grumpy sleepy whiny
        I need a nap
        I lost my doll
        You give me that ball
        You get out of my hair
            time of the afternoon
When everyone is tired
        of everyone else
When all the voices
        are jangly

That's just when Aunt Dena raises her hand
                and starts to lead
                    the family band
And we grab for pot-lid cymbals
                    plastic bucket drums
                    spoons and rattles
                    whistles and maracas
                    claves and kazoos
Around the park we march
            weaving in and out of the shady trees
                    clanging and banging
                    weeting and tweeting
                        loud and proud
perfectly out-of-tune
            and perfectly in harmony

SEARCHING FOR BEAVERS

Not one of us has ever seen a beaver
      on Beaverdam Lake
But still we search
      every year
            patrolling the pond
            in our faded blue pedal boats

Ducks we see
Gulls, too, by the score
Elegant mute swans
      iceberg white
      with their flotilla of cygnets
        sooty as city snow
Funny little grebes
      popping up from under the water
        like winning number ping-pong balls
        in a contest on TV
But never a buck-toothed paddle-tailed
        beaver
Not one

So today we are amazed

  when Frankie cries, "There. Look, there!"

And we all pedal wildly

  spinning thrashing eventually crashing

to converge on one hairy brown shape

  in the middle of the lake

"But where are the buck teeth?

  "Where is the tail?" asks Bobby

"And why doesn't it move?" adds Jon

And we are sad

  mourning the death

    of our first and only

      beaver

when Uncle Bill fishes it out warily
      with just his fingertips
and we see it's not a beaver at all
      but a stringy scruffy waterlogged
          wig
"Ooh, icky," squeals Tasha
      as Cousin Jon snatches it
      and Uncle Dan catches it
      and over our heads it soars
              lands
      again and again   squish-splat
      from boat to boat to boat
By the end of the day the lake becomes
      Piggywig Pond
and not one of us can hear the word
      beaver
    without laughing
    laughing
    laughing

POSSE

In his Lone Ranger T-shirt
     Great-Uncle Nicholas gallops
all around the baseball field
     spurring on his speedy wheelchair
        with a "Hi-ho, Silver! Away!"

Just when I think I'm too old to join him
     here I am again
        right after Jon and Tasha and Baby Ben
        riding shotgun in his lap
"There they are—
     Hard-hearted Bart and Willy the Kid!" he shouts

He tells me what they look like
        from the tip of their spurs
                to the top of their ten-gallon hats
"One hundred yards. Fifty yards. Thirty yards, and gaining!" he yells
        "Get out the lasso. Get out the lariat.
        Hold on tight. We'll get them yet!"

And as we race through the dust around the diamond
        I swear our seat becomes a saddle
                our wheels a horse's hooves
                and the field a rich green prairie
                where rabbits run for cover
                and buffalo still roam

CLOSINGS

Nothing disturbs Dad more
    than a restaurant at closing time
        when they start to stack
            the chairs on the tables
        and put all the milk pitchers away
    or the last movie show
        when they sweep up
            the popcorn in the sticky aisles
        and turn out the lights on the marquee
It's that left alone get out of here go home feeling
    Dad can't stand
So, long before the sun's set
    and the next to last car has left the parking lot
we begin our good-byes
    packing up the bats and balls
        and the picnic basket
    collecting the suntan oil from Aunt Laura
        the tablecloth from Baby Ben
    patting and hugging and saying
        See you tomorrow
            to Grandma Rita

        See you on Tuesday
            to Cousin Jon

        See you next year
            to Great-Uncle Nicholas
            to Aunt Amelia
            to Max's Grandma Deborah
            to Carrie and to George

Then we're walking and waving
           walking and waving

      exiting through the grass and trees

          to the asphalt

      alongside Aunt Rebecca

          who's due to have a baby

            maybe any day

When we reach the car

      Dad lets out a sigh

      and Mom wipes at her eye

      and I call out the window one final good-bye

          to my family

            that's always different
               always changing

      and to Small Park

     that's always pretty
      much
        the same

THE MORNING AFTER LABOR DAY

The morning after Labor Day
  we hear them test the school bell
and even Dad is sad
  knowing summer will soon be lost
   in the shuffle of new shoes
    notebooks
    pencil cases
     we'll lose by Thanksgiving
Then the photograph comes in the mail
  and we are smack-dab back
   in the middle of summer
   and Small Park
There's Bobby in his baseball cap
  Aunt Alicia in her blue silk dress
   Baby Ben waving
  Cousin George raving
   Carrie, Frankie, Uncle Steve
  all the grandmas, Max and me
Sixty-two of us
  smiling at Grandpa Jerry's camera
  smiling in the sunshine
   we wish would never end
"Quite a family," Dad whistles
  "You bet it is," Mom grins
And I proudly prop the picture on top of the TV
  to admire like a trophy
   that all of us have won